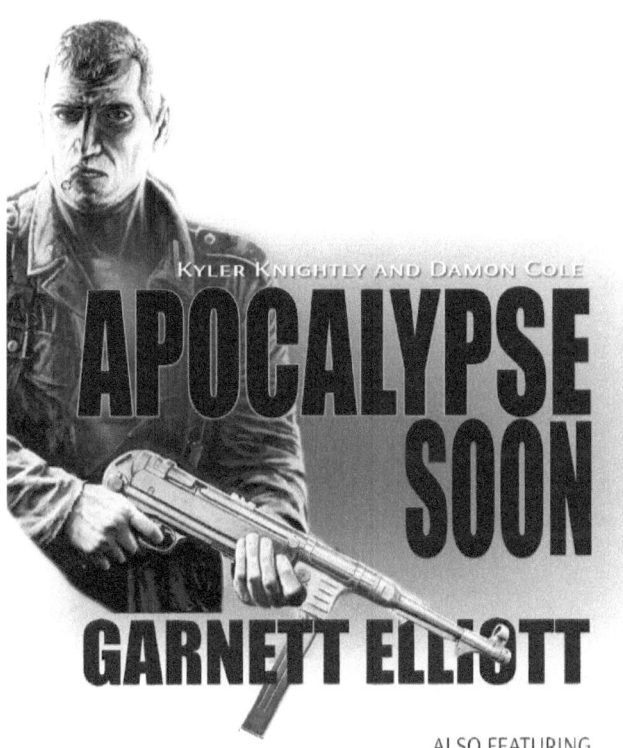

KYLER KNIGHTLY AND DAMON COLE

APOCALYPSE SOON

GARNETT ELLIOTT

ALSO FEATURING
BABYLON HEIST
A KYLER KNIGHTLY AND DAMON COLE ADVENTURE

WITH BONUS SCI-FI SHORT
STRONTIUM DREAMS

www.beattoapulp.com

For the First KNIGHTLY AND COLE Adventures

FROM BEAT TO A PULP BOOKS
www.beattoapulp.com

It's a dirty job ...

Policing the timelines has always been danger-ous, but the brave agents of Continuity Inc. have arguably the most important job in human history. Protecting human history.

Newly promoted agent Kyler Knightly teams up with his uncle, Damon Cole, to stop unscrupu-lous developers from ex-ploiting the Late Cretaceous. A luxury subdivision smack-dab in the middle of dinosaur country threatens not only the present, but super-rich homeowners looking for the ultimate getaway.

CARNOSAUR WEEKEND includes the original Kyler Knightly story "The Zygma Gambit," inspired by the dream journals of Kyle J. Knapp, and a sci-fi short story "The Worms of Terpsichore," all together totaling nearly 16K words.

CONTENTS

"If time travel is possible, where are the tourists from the future?"

—Stephen Hawking
A Brief History of Time

APOCALYPSE SOON

The warning klaxon sounded just as Kyler Knightly set down his tray of chamomile tea and shortbread. At twenty-three hundred hours, he was the only person in the Continuity Inc. canteen.

So much for a late night snack.

He bolted towards the exit, his skin still itching after a recent jaunt to Panama, circa 1913, to save the Canal from time-hopping anarchists. No one had briefed him about the goddamn mosquitos. He'd had to spend hours in the infirmary afterwards, submitting to the robotic ministrations of the Derm-o-Doc.

Technicians hustled past in the hall. "Knightly!" called a feminine voice.

Melody Fischer came sprinting over. The top of her short dark hair only came up to his chest, though nobody ever kidded about her height. In addition to being a field agent, she served as Continuity Inc.'s aikido instructor.

"What's going on?" he said.

"Rogue jaunt. That's the buzz, anyway."

They hurried to the auditorium. Kyler's uncle Damon Cole, puffy-eyed from sleep, was already on stage. He'd just finished wheeling out Continuity's AI in a large Flexiglas tank. Kyler forgot about his itching skin. There must be something truly bad in the offing, to bring Sennacherib II all the way down from his fourth-floor suite.

"Where is everybody?" Fischer said, looking around.

Damon shrugged broad shoulders. "We three are it. Our Strike Team jaunted off to Ceres two hours ago, and no one knows when they'll be back."

"Great timing," Kyler said.

Sennacherib's chip-voice rattled from speakers attached to his tank. "The timing is no coincidence. Fellow sentients, we have a traitor in our midst. A Continuity technician has gone rogue."

"Who?" Kyler said.

Sennacherib's tentacles brushed a control pad. In order to make AI's more empathic, newer models were surgically implanted inside animals. Sennacherib shared headspace with a California two-spot octopus. At his touch, a holo sprang up above the tank. It depicted the bust of a middle aged man, non-descript save for a certain glaze to his eyes.

"Paul Dirac," Sennacherib said. "Master technician in R and D, and up until ten minutes ago a rules-abiding employee. Spotless record. Per the company shrink, he has an obsession with Pre-Apocalypse North America and vintage automobiles. Quirky, though that's to be expected with a genius IQ."

"Where'd he jaunt to?"

"Take a look around the stage. The answer should be obvious."

Furniture and props had been placed to form a crude set. Hastily done, but serviceable. Shelves lined with canned vegetables, tinned meat, how-to books and packets of freeze dried coffee. A water purifier. Several shotguns.

"I'd guess this is a survivalist's room," Fischer said, examining a can of peaches. "An underground shelter, maybe. If Dirac's obsessed with the Pre-Apocalypse era …"

Sennacherib's bulbous head nodded. "Excellent deduction. Given the Zygma projector's last settings, I estimate a high probability the jaunt's destination was an area known as Old Vegas, circa 2035. A dangerous and pivotal time in American history. The mass indicator shows Dirac jaunted back with a substantial amount of supplies. You'll need to go after him, stat."

Damon held up a hand. "Whoa, now. Give us a chance to get strapped, first."

"Quickly. There's no telling how much damage an insider could do to the time-stream."

Damon rushed offstage to return moments later with a flat black case. Nestled inside were a trio of flechette pistols. He pocketed one for himself and doled out the remainder. Kyler caught Fischer eyeing his uncle's muscular torso as he handed her a pistol.

"Observe some restraint, please," Sennacherib said. "We want Dirac brought back alive, if possible."

"What're we using for focus objects?" Kyler said.

"Everything on the set is a certified antique, so take whatever looks portable."

Kyler grabbed the closest thing; a slanted cross made from chrome, wider than it was tall. Damon, predictably, chose a shotgun, and Fischer selected a tiny can opener.

They were ready.

"Twenty-first century English is close enough to contemporary Anglic," Sennacherib said, "so you shouldn't need a voder. Does everyone have recall beacons? Good. Now find your marks."

Humming echoed through the auditorium as a Zygma projector came sliding in stage left, its faceted quartz "eye" already starting to spin. Kyler clenched his gut out of reflex; jaunts usually meant an attack of nausea. How many did this make for him now? Two dozen? He'd lost count.

Stage lights flickered and dimmed. The Zygma process drew horrendous amounts of power, straining every spare erg from the fission pile in the basement. The quartz eye spun faster, faster. Pallid radiation streamed out over the three agents.

Damon grinned. "Quickest briefing we ever had, huh?"

The image of his smile froze in place, as Zygma particles unknit the surrounding reality. In moments they would be wrenched from London's West End and sent hurling through the chronosphere.

A screech replaced the background humming. Damon's image wavered, obscured by a shower of violet sparks.

4

Something was wrong.

Dirac must've known they'd be coming after him. He must've—

Blackness.

*　*　*

—*sabotaged the projector.*

Kyler materialized ankle-deep in a rippling sand dune. Hot, desiccated wind threw grit in his face. He fought the urge to dry heave as his senses reoriented, logic pointing out that yes, the big blazing ball overhead was the sun, and further, he was breathing unassisted, with just the right amount of pressure bearing down on his skin.

So he'd materialized on Earth. And not within a volcano or at the bottom of the Marianas Trench. He had that going for him. *When* he was remained a question, however.

Low mountains huddled in the distance. Even closer, sunlight gleamed off a bizarre cityscape, not quite in ruins. A replica of the Eiffel Tower leaned at a dangerous angle, not far from a pyramid made of black glass. Between them sprawled multi-storied buildings, dry pools and cracked fountains that ran with dust instead of water.

Old Vegas.

Maybe Dirac's sabotage had been too hurried to truly screw them over. This seemed like the right time period. And he *would* be in a hurry, trying to jaunt before security caught him. Hope sparked. "Damon?" he called out. "Fischer?"

His voice broke into echoes.

Alright, that might've been too optimistic. Still, the chance remained his fellow agents were around here, somewhere, contemporaneous to him. He had to believe that. The thought of Uncle Damon materializing in hard vacuum …

He shuffled down the dune. For a moment he contemplated using his recall beacon, but ditched the idea. If the projector was damaged, he might not be so lucky on his jaunt back. Better to wait.

By instinct he headed towards the ruined city. If this was indeed somewhen around 2035, the Slow Fall of North America had only recently begun. Major infrastructure should still be intact. Ergo, the city might have a community living somewhere inside it. How they would react to strangers wandering in from the desert was anyone's guess, however.

He felt for the flechette pistol's comforting grip.

Fifteen minutes later he reached a strip of weathered asphalt. A vehicle had been parked off the shoulder. Seeing it brought another hopeful twinge. The vehicle was clearly a gascar, of a subtype known as a 'pickup truck.' Hulking, with oversized tires, the bed sported a heavy machinegun on a gyro mount. Aluminum spikes jutted from the sides.

No one was at the wheel or close by. If the truck had been abandoned, it must've happened recently. The cab door hung open. He approached, trying to remember how twenty-first century ignition systems worked. Something about a key—

"Hands high!"

A patch of sand to the truck's right thrust upwards, and a rifle barrel poked out. Eyes glinted behind it. Kyler raised his empty hands.

"That's good. Porkchop, frisk him."

"Don't need to," came a voice from somewhere behind the truck. "I can see his gun clear as day."

"Go and take it off him, then."

Sighs. An obese man in desert camo waddled around the truck bed. He must've been hiding on the other side. His gelled hair stuck up in a rooster's comb, and he wore goggles with darkened lenses. A trench knife hung from his belt, but he didn't draw it as he approached.

"Hey, mister," said the rifleman, "you got any friends with you?"

"It's just me," Kyler said.

"Try anything and I'll light you up."

Porkchop tore the flechette pistol from his pocket. "What the hell's this? Some kind of toy? It's made of plastic."

"Let me see." The gunman climbed out of his hiding place. He wore similar fatigues, surprisingly clean for someone who'd been crouching in a hole, and had gone to the trouble of painting his face with elaborate makeup. Sweat had already smeared the design into a colorful blob.

Porkchop tossed the pistol over. The gunman caught it with his free hand, the other keeping the rifle trained on Kyler. "Looks pretty wussified to me. Check him for more goodies."

Thick fingers brushed over Kyler's coveralls. They found the strange focus object in his breast pocket and drew it out. Both men uttered respectful gasps.

"Whoa," said Porkchop. "Factory original, it looks like."

"Where'd you get this?" said the gunman.

"It's, ah, mine. Family heirloom."

Chrome winked as Porkchop held up the wide cross. After a moment's admiration he handed it back.

"That's a holy symbol, mister," said the gunman, squinting at Kyler's face. "Where you from, anyway? You're too pale to be a local. Ah, skip it. I can guess. You've come wandering out here to hook up with the Clark County Militia, haven't you? Only reason you'd be on foot, carrying that."

"I'm looking for a man named Dirac," Kyler said. "Have either of you—"

"*Father* Dirac," Porkchop corrected.

"Of course you're looking for him," said the gunman. "We're all looking for him. And that sweet, sweet ride he's offering at the rally tonight."

Porkchop rested his hands on his ample hips. "We can't waste this guy, Two Wyck. Not if he wants to convert."

"Agreed. You *do* want to convert, don't you, bud?"

Kyler nodded with enthusiasm.

"Awesome. Well, we'll take you back to camp. My name's Two Wyck Ed, by the way. Get it? Too wicked? You'll probably want to be thinking of a Militia handle too, instead of whatever lame-ass name your mama gave you."

"Can I have my gun back?"

"Sorry. I know it sounds kind of blasphemous, but you can't bear arms until you pass our initiation. Then it'll be cool."

Loud static burst from the truck's cab, followed by a high-pitched tone. The two men exchanged looks.

"That's the emergency frequency," Porkchop said.

"No shit. Go turn it up."

They hustled over to the cab. Porkchop fiddled with the dials of what looked like a CB radio hung below the dash.

"… all units. There's a convoy on the juice-line up from Barstow. Repeat, convoy traveling I-15. Multiple civilian vehicles and cargo. At least one heavy rig, so watch your ass. All units, please respond …"

"Hot damn," Porkchop said.

"Man your post." Two Wyck grinned at Kyler. "Looks like we get to bust your cherry early. Take shotgun."

"What do you mean—?"

"*Move it.*"

Ammunition boxes formed a barrier between the seats. Kyler had to clamber around the truck's front to reach the passenger side. He saw something attached to the grill, just below the hood.

It was the strange cross symbol.

* * *

Two Wyck buried the accelerator. Desert landscape sped past in a russet blur. From the primitive gauges on the dash, Kyler guessed their speed was in excess of a hundred-sixty kilometers per hour. He tried to focus on that, and not the horrid, twangy music playing over the roar of the air conditioner.

"Like it?" Two Wyck said. "That's from Country Thunder '17. They sure knew how to auto-tune back then. Not like the crap we get now."

Porkchop rode in the truck bed. He stuck his goggled face through a small back window. "You worried about that rig, boss?"

"Only thing I'm worried about is if the Elko Preppers get there first. Look sharp, now. We're nearing the highway."

Two Wyck eased off the gas. A larger strip of road appeared to their left, and as he swerved onto it a mongrel line of cars and vans filled the driver's side window. Porkchop let out a war-whoop.

"Look at that herd," Two Wyck said. "Easy pickings."

He started to accelerate, bearing down on a squat red van. A fireball blossomed directly ahead. Two Wyck swerved around it, nearly flipping the truck.

"What the hell was that?"

"Preppers," shouted Porkchop. "I see 'em. One o'clock."

A dirt bike bearing two riders had leapt onto the road some twenty meters in front of them. The rearmost rider lofted a bottle with a flaming rag stuffed into the neck. Porkchop opened up. Bullets stitched pavement around the bike, tearing chunks of asphalt before finding the gas tank. And both riders. The bike shuddered with multiple impacts and turned into a second geyser of fire, easily avoided.

"Watch the goddamn ammo," Two Wyck shouted.

A gray behemoth loomed in the window at eleven o'clock. The aforementioned heavy rig, slowing down to protect its charges. Armor bulged along the sides of the trailer, and a bubble turret, bristling with twin guns, protruded from the top. Two Wyck swore and tapped the brakes, just as the turret poured a fusillade of tracer rounds. His reflexes saved the truck from being cut down the middle. Accelerating again, he swerved behind the cover a nearby van. The tracers didn't follow.

"Sum*bitch*," he said, fuming at no one in particular. His makeup was running in a torrent now, the bright red and blue smearing into sweaty gray.

Behind the pickup came the whine of high-revving engines. Dune buggies shot past on either side. They'd been affixed with the same spikes and gun mounts as the pickup, and the leftmost sported what looked like a mortar tube. The driver on the right flipped them off as he passed.

"Our boys," Two Wyck said. "They sure took their sweet time. But they'll grab all the glory if we don't hurry."

He swerved back out from cover. The rightmost buggy was already blazing away, marching a stream of slugs into the rig's oversized tires. Tread puckered, but didn't blow. Solid rubber. The turret answered fire, with more effective results: tracers chewed the buggy's cab to shreds, and Two Wyck had to execute a hard left to avoid the smoking remains.

"Porkchop! Top that turret!"

A hollow *whump* sounded to their left. Kyler caught the glare of a mortar round arcing upwards, to alight seconds later atop the truck. The bubble turret disappeared in a burst of incandescent flame. Two Wyck hollered and slammed on the gas.

They sped alongside the big rig, Porkchop bouncing rounds off the sloped armor. A panel slid back and a helmeted figure leaned out with an assault rifle. Porkchop's .50 pulped his face. Two Wyck, in the spirit of things now, rolled down the window as he drew alongside the rig's cab. He aimed the flechette pistol and squeezed off several rounds. Humming darts struck sparks from the armor.

"No-penetration piece of shit." He tossed the gun out the window.

"Boss," Porkchop shouted, "whatever they're haulin's too hard to get. Let's score something easy."

"Good idea."

Two Wyck cut speed behind the now-toothless rig, and drew up on the red van he'd chosen before. It was pulling a cargo pod on a small trailer. As the pickup came parallel, lining up for a good shot, Kyler caught a glimpse of the family inside. Two parents, two kids, and a dog. The father hunched over the wheel, focused on his driving, while the white-faced mother wrestled a SMG into firing position. The children watched with dull eyes.

"Sayonara, suckers," Two Wyck said.

Enough. Kyler reached over, grabbed the steering wheel, and yanked.

At one hundred thirty kilometers per hour, the pickup spun into a roll. It corkscrewed off the freeway like some nightmare amusement ride. Kyler had taken the precaution earlier of buckling into his four-point harness. Two Wyck hadn't. He smacked against the roof. Against the dash. The pickup lost inertia and went sliding sideways, flipped over. Dust enveloped the cracked windows.

Kyler hung upside down like a bat. Beside him, Two Wyck groaned. Blood poured from his cut scalp, adding fresh red to the makeup mess. He managed to cock his head towards Kyler. "You'll never … never get into the militia now …"

Kyler popped the harness. He dropped down and managed to land on his shoulder. An ammo box lay to one side; he grabbed it up and slammed it against Two Wyck's head with all his strength. The driver slumped. Dead or unconscious, Kyler didn't care.

He got the door open. Dust still swirled. One of Porkchop's thick legs stuck out from beneath the truck bed. He must've held on instead of being thrown. Kyler hunkered down and took a quick look at the mangled body underneath.

The dune buggy with the mortar appeared through the haze. It braked and three people got out; two men in desert camo, leading a short woman bound at the wrists. Kyler's breath caught.

It was Fischer. Dusty, with a bruise along her jaw, but still vertical.

One of the men pointed a machine pistol at Kyler. "What the fuck happened to Two Wyck's rig? And who the fuck are you?"

Think fast. "Ah, a convert? Two Wyck was going to take me to meet Father Dirac, at the rally tonight."

"So what happened?"

"He lost control of his pickup."

The man shook his head. "Bullshit. Two Wyck's one of our best drivers."

"I'm afraid he might be dead. Porkchop is for sure."

The dust had settled. Porkchop's errant leg stuck out for everyone to see. Kyler felt like he'd been caught at a crime scene. He glanced at Fischer, who gave him a slow wink.

"I'm in no mood for games right now," said the man with the pistol, "so we'll—"

Fischer swept his ankle. He went down face first into the sand, and she stomped his wrist. *Crack.* The second man reached to unshoulder his rifle. Her little foot found his groin, chambered back, and snap-kicked him under the chin. He toppled. Somehow she'd kept her balance the whole time.

Kyler rushed over. "He's got my flechette in his right pocket," she said, nodding towards the first man. Kyler dug the gun out and put a narco round apiece in both their backs. Paralytic toxins did the rest.

"If I'd known aikido was that effective," he said, "I would've spent more time in practice."

She managed a grin. "Tae Kwon Do, actually. Works better when you're bound."

"I've got just the thing for that." Kyler returned to the truck and took the trench knife from Porkchop's bloodied hip. The serrated blade made short work of Fischer's bindings.

"Now what?" she said.

He surveyed the highway. The convoy, with its attendant predators, was long gone. Only the smell of cordite and diesel remained. "Tell me what happened to you."

"Same thing that happened to you, it looks like. Dirac must've screwed with the Zygma projector. I appeared in the middle of the desert and wandered until these two morons grabbed me."

"Did you see any sign of Damon?"

"Nope, but if you and I found each other this quick he shouldn't be far."

A comforting thought. "The two guys I was with called Dirac 'Father.' I get the impression he's set up some sort of cult here."

"Which means we didn't appear hot on his heels."

"No. The projector sent us to the right place, but the wrong time. I'd guess Dirac's been here for months, at least." He nodded towards the dune buggy. "Let's take that and go looking for Damon. The idiot who captured me mentioned a rally tonight, where Dirac's supposed to appear. We can look for that, too."

"Sounds like a plan."

He took the machine pistol from the prone man's broken grip. Come to think of it, his desert fatigues might come in handy, too. Kyler's own Continuity uniform would stick out in a crowd.

"Ah, do you mind?" he said, loosening the buttons on his coveralls.

Fischer snorted as she turned around. "Don't worry, slim. I wasn't planning on watching."

* * *

They took the buggy over rolling hills, past the remnants of subdivisions given to sand. Stucco mansions in neat rows. They were behemoths by twenty-third century standards, and still intact. While Kyler drove, Fischer found an ample supply of bottled water and beef jerky between the seats. The jerky came in bright commercial packaging; it wasn't homemade.

"What the hell happened here?" she said, chewing. "I thought this was supposed to be the apocalypse."

"*Pre*-apocalypse, remember? North America hasn't collapsed yet." He turned onto a residential road. "Not completely, anyway. And what happened here is drought."

"So why are all these nuts shooting people like its Armageddon?"

"Because they want to. The survivalists of this period got tired of waiting for End Times. Plus, there's no public law enforcement left to stop them."

Fischer shook her head. "Anarchy."

"'Freedom,' the way they see it."

He slowed. Another walled subdivision was coming up on the left, but this one looked inhabited. There were metal gates and gun emplacements. Waning afternoon sun glinted off the panels of a greenhouse, tucked inside. A banner stretched across the wall read:

WARNING! PROTECTED BY THE RANCHO VISTA H.O.A. THIS MEANS YOU, MOTHERFUCKER!

A bullet kicked up sand two meters in front of them. Kyler waved to the unseen sniper and turned the buggy around.

* * *

No sign of Damon.

They drove until the fuel gauge crept towards empty. Kyler tried to avoid other vehicles, but as the sun slipped behind the horizon he spotted a line of cars and trucks threading around a small mountain, making for a concrete ring in the distance.

"I bet that's your rally," Fischer said.

"If Dirac's there, Damon might be, too. Anyways, this could be the only chance to nab our rogue."

He drove to the rear of the line. The vehicle in front was a flatbed truck hauling about a dozen scruffy men and women. They wore plastic shin guards and shoulder pads, their heads covered by hooded green jerseys. Some had a chrome emblem with archaic lettering on chains around their necks. They glared venom at Kyler and Fischer, but made no move to jump down from the truck.

"I don't think they like us," Fischer said.

"A rival militia group. Probably the 'Elko Preppers' my associates were going on about." He fished the cross symbol out of his pocket and showed it to her. "This is some kind of cult object, based on antique vehicles."

Fischer smirked. "You sound like an anthropologist."

"Not a lot of call for that in the field."

The line moved at a good pace. A little farther down, a battered sign read: LAS VEGAS MOTOR SPEEDWAY. Vehicles were being waved off the road to park in rows along the hard-packed sand. Kyler followed suit. A man in a brown monk's habit directed them towards a second line of foot traffic. They filed through a gate, where another monk was taking guns and exchanging them for tickets. The weapons were tagged and placed in a fortified trailer, presumably to be returned later. No one seemed happy about the exchange. Kyler gave up his gun, but Fischer, saying nothing about the flechette in her boot, passed through a metal detector without it going off.

Inside, a massive crowd milled around an equally massive racetrack. Roaring engines competed with the hoarse voices of vendors, hawking bottled beer, bags of popcorn, and something called 'survival dogs'—rat carcasses roasted over a propane fire. On closer inspection, Kyler saw the 'rats' were actually made from pressed turkey. Or so a sign assured him. He felt no urge to verify.

Sodium lights flickered to life above. Fischer grabbed Kyler by the hand and shoved through the crowd. They reached a chain link fence encircling the track, a bowl-shaped depression with all the action going on in the center. Only two vehicles remained among a jumble of smoking wrecks, and they weren't racing. A low slung sedan circled an armored school bus painted hot pink. The sedan snapped off bursts from hood-mounted machineguns as it caught angles on the less agile bus.

Somebody nudged Kyler. "Hey pal, you need to take a leak?"

He turned to see a bald man carrying a clear plastic tank slung over his back. A hose with a broad funnel at one end connected to the tank, already full of frothy urine.

"It's for the Piss of Shame," the man said, by way of explanation. "Should be coming up real soon."

"He'll pass, thank you," Fischer said.

"Suit yourself." The man handed Kyler a sweating bottle of beer. "You look like you need one of these, son. On the house." He hurried off.

Despite himself, Kyler took a long pull.

In the arena, the pink bus was fighting back. A tongue of flame lanced from an open window and engulfed the sedan's cab as it roared past. Napalm licked away paint and primer. Blinded, the sedan struck a charred pickup, caromed off like a billiard ball, and ran headlong into the sloping side of the arena. Fans nearby shrieked approval as they bolted for cover. The resulting explosion rained hot metal into the crowd.

A tow rig came out to clear away the wreckage, while the bus spun victory doughnuts. At the far end of the track, a pair of giant digital screens flickered to life. Dirac's face peered out at the multitudes. He'd grown a full beard, and his eyes had changed from glazed to stone-crazy. At sight of him the whole raceway drew a collective breath. The bus stopped spinning.

Dirac's voice rumbled out over PA speakers.

"Far back in America's past, when the Cult of the Car was still young, Eddie Olson and Tyrone Baker raced Ford and Chevy for the first time."

Cheers from the crowd. Dirac spoke with a passion he'd never shown as a reclusive R and D tech.

"Their holy rivalry continues to this day. In these End Times, as our diseased society shudders closer to its death rattle, we enact the rites of old, not by racing, but through purifying combat."

"Yeah," someone catcalled nearby. "So get back to the combat, already."

"We want 'splosions!"

Dirac continued: "Tonight, the drivers of the Clark County Militia square off against their longtime foes, the Elko Preppers. Chevy versus Ford. So far, Elko's Pink Flambeaux has prevailed, but the final match is yet to come. And the prize ..."

The rightmost screen changed view, showing a hand held shot of a small pickup. Ooh's and ahh's echoed through the crowd. A collective licking of lips. The camera zoomed in on various features as Dirac spoke. "A low pro custom mini from '22. Yes, that's purple neon on the rims. It's got Alpine full-surround, and those testicles hanging from the hitch are thirty-two ounces of pure Sterling. Will a bowtie or a Ford go on the hood? It's still up for grabs."

"But that's not the best part, ladies and gentlemen." The screen changed again, filling with a shot of a large metal statue high in the grandstands. Strangely, the statue depicted a boy with a large head of spiky hair.

He'd pulled his shorts down in preparation to urinate. His penis, Kyler noted with confusion, was a spigot.

"Tonight, the Piss of Shame will not rain down on Ford or Chevy emblem alone. No. Tonight we're mixing concentrated battery acid in with the collection. Enough to melt the skin off our lovely human sacrifices, captured fresh from the wastelands this afternoon."

The screen zoomed down to show a dark-haired woman in a leather dress, manacled to a slab. Two cowled figures in monks' habits hovered over her. The screen panned left to show a similarly manacled male wearing leather briefs. Kyler recognized him even before the camera caught his bearded face.

"Holy shit," Fischer said.

"Which way will the burning Piss of Shame fall?" boomed Dirac. "Will it be Elko, and the woman? Or Clark County and the man? Ford or Chevy. Fate has yet to decide."

"It'll be neither," Kyler said.

Fischer pursed her lips, surveying the half mile of crowd stretching between them and the grandstands. "How're we getting up there?"

"We start moving, now. There might still be time."

On the giant screen, Dirac's face grew florid and spittle flew as he introduced Hung Low, the reigning Clark County champion, a black truck with tires so monstrously huge the cab rode four meters high. A long, spiked shaft protruded from beneath the chassis. A battering ram? But Kyler had to focus his attention on the crowd, slipping between bodies.

They worked their way closer to the grandstands. At midpoint Kyler stopped cold and grabbed Fischer to do likewise. His nape tingled a warning. He sensed more than saw the man staring at him from several meters away.

Two Wyck Ed gnawed a faux rat, the left side of his head bandaged. Next to him stood the badly sunburned driver of the mortar buggy.

"*Move*." Kyler gave Fischer a shove.

But Two Wyck was pointing now, shouting "traitor." Heads turned. Half the crowd were Clark County Militia, and they'd be swarming in seconds. Kyler turned to the closest Elko Prepper, a bearded man in a green jersey, and smacked his half-full beer against his forehead. The Prepper went careening into a Militia member.

"Free for all!" Fischer shouted. She grabbed another Prepper and hip-threw him at the charging Two Wyck. Both men went down in a tussle.

Kyler dove beneath a pair of legs and scooted behind a popcorn stand. Fischer joined him seconds later. The spectators' adrenalin, already on edge from the arena fighting, found expression as brawling erupted.

"Good move," Fischer said. "But how're we going to get through this mess now?"

Kyler pointed at the fence surrounding the track. "Climb. There's no crowd in the arena. When we get closer to the grandstands we can climb back over."

"But the cars—"

He didn't wait for her approval. All he could think of was battery acid eating his uncle's face. He reached the chain link and started scrambling up it. People shouted, but most attention was elsewhere. A thrown bottle missed his head. He got to the top, scrambled over, and started down the other side. Fischer followed, agile as a monkey.

They leapt down onto asphalt. Forty meters away, pink bus and black monster truck were circling. The bus trundled near.

"Run," Fischer said.

They raced along the edge of the track. The bus swiped past, a pink blur with faces pressed against the windows. Napalm's burnt-grease smell filled Kyler's nostrils.

They ran on, heedless. The grandstands loomed close. There was a nearby shriek of metal on metal; Hung Low had crashed into the bus from behind and rolled up partly over it, mounting it like an animal. The battering ram swung back. Pistons hissed, slamming the spiked tip through pink metal.

Fischer ignored the crowd's feral howls. "I can see the statue over there. We're close."

They clambered back over the fence. Brawling between Elko and Clark County had yet to reach the crowd here, who were too enthralled by the bus-fucking to pay much attention as Kyler and Fischer leapt down. They shoved their way up to the grandstands, past better-dressed spectators in designer camo suits.

"How do we get to the statue?" Kyler said.

"Dunno. I don't see ... wait."

Kyler spotted it too, set back among the bleachers. A door marked STAFF ONLY, flanked by two cowled figures. The platform with the statue was directly above. Both monks clutched short carbines with bell-shaped barrels.

"Screamers," Kyler said. "Dirac must've brought those back with him. Great for crowd control."

"I brought something back, too." Fischer slipped the pistol out of her boot.

"Wait."

The monks seemed engrossed as everyone else, but the cowls hiding their faces made it difficult to tell. Below, in the arena, the Pink Flambeaux had finally brought a flamethrower to bear. Orange-white brilliance arced from a rear window and melted one of Hung Low's oversized tires.

"*Now*," Kyler said.

Fischer fired from the hip. On full auto, a stream of tranq darts struck the first monk, his body already slumping as she walked the burst into the second. Crowd noises swallowed the pistol's hum.

Kyler snatched a screamer from nerveless fingers, shouldered the door, and pulled Fischer through without looking to see who might've noticed. He threw the door's bolt behind them. They hunkered in a narrow stairwell leading up.

Fischer motioned. Together, they crept on either side of the stairs, their backs to the walls. Fischer burst out left and Kyler took right.

They'd emerged onto a railed platform overlooking the stands. At the center stood the giant spiky-haired boy, his metal spigot poised within splashing distance of Damon and the dark-haired woman. A trio of monks were hauling buckets up a ladder, where they dumped the foamy contents into a reservoir at the statue's back. A fourth monk holding a submachine gun looked on.

Fischer's pistol swung towards the gunner. Kyler leveled the screamer at the remaining monks and pressed the firing stud.

His teeth shivered in their sockets. A wave of sound knocked over the ladder, dropped the monks and their buckets. Blood spurted from noses and ears. He shut the weapon off before sonic waves shuddered their brains to gel.

Fischer, meanwhile, dropped her man. With no other guards in sight, Kyler rushed to where his uncle lay.

"About goddamn time." Damon tried to crane his head up from the slab, but shackles held him back. Like Fischer, he'd been bruised around the jaw and temples.

"Nice briefs." Kyler couldn't hide a grin.

"Tell anyone about this and I swear …"

Kyler gave the shackles an experimental tug. "The keys are over there," Damon said, "on the gunman. Get 'em fast, and get me his weapon."

But Fischer was already headed over with key ring in hand. She waggled her eyebrows at Damon. "Well now, I think the leather look suits you."

"Stop screwing around. We've got to get the woman free before it' pissing time."

Kyler unlocked his uncle's bonds. The dark-haired woman, sluggish as if she'd been doped on something, took a little longer. He dragged her a healthy distance from the spigot, while Damon grabbed the fallen monk's SMG. He found a jacket and jeans beneath the brown robes, and slipped them on.

"I'm going after Dirac. There's another ladder behind the statue, leading to a press box. He's up there."

"Huh-uh," Fischer said. "You're wounded."

Damon patted the jacket pockets, discovered a cigar stub. "You don't look so great yourself."

"*I'll* go," Kyler said. "Uncle, you cover the stairwell. The door's bolted at the bottom, but it won't hold back a mob if they decide to rush us."

Damon rolled the stub around in his mouth. "You sure you're up for this?"

"I'm an agent now, remember? I've got to take risks like everyone else."

He found the ladder and started climbing, before he changed his mind. With the screamer slung over his shoulder, he clambered up the rungs. Below stretched the grandstand crowd. He forced himself to forget about them, and the hundred-meter height. The little square of trapdoor above was the only thing that mattered. Vibration on the rungs made him look down; Fischer was following. He motioned for her to go back. She shook her head, her face resolute.

No use arguing. He reached the trapdoor and poked his head through. The flared muzzle of a screamer pointed at him. Behind it, Dirac's grin split his bearded face.

"First the uncle, now the nephew. I figured Continuity would be sending someone, sooner or later."

He had a live mike clipped to his robes, and his voice boomed out over the PA system. It didn't seem to bother him. "Come up slowly," he said, backing away. "Try anything untoward and I'll give you a full-power burst. At this range it'll liquefy your skull."

Kyler crawled into the press box, keeping his hands free from the butt of his weapon. He didn't dare look down at Fischer. This high up the wind blew cold and the night sky blazed. Dirac leaned against the bulk of a television camera. "You might've tried a quieter way of taking out my monks," he said. "Besides Damon, how many more of you are there?"

"Just us two," Kyler lied. "The Strike Team was away when you jaunted."

Dirac chewed on that.

"Why'd you do it, Paul? Why'd you go rogue?"

"I'm not sure your twenty-third century mind can comprehend my reasons. You're too comfortable, too coddled by the 'civilized' world. Also, you're not a gearhead."

"All I see here are a bunch of stupid people reverting to barbarism."

"*Exactly*." Dirac's eyes shone. "Man's natural state. Not that puerile and overpopulated mess you're used to, back in the present. Imagine: two tribes locked in constant warfare, laying rubber across the face of history. The eternal dualism of Ford versus Chevy. Every major town in the U.S. has a racetrack like this one, just waiting to be turned into an arena. Europe, too. The cult will spread, and spread …"

Kyler thought he heard a shuffling below. He kept his eyes fixed on Dirac. "Continuity will keep sending back agents. You must know that."

"Not if I change history fast enough. There won't *be* a Continuity Inc., at this rate."

Beneath them came a staccato burst of automatic fire. Dirac glanced down. In the same moment Fischer popped her head, and the barrel of her flechette pistol, up through the trapdoor. No good: Dirac's screamer could pulp them both before she'd have time to aim.

Kyler leapt forward. He managed to grab Dirac's carbine in both hands. A blast of sound shot sideways, striking a camera and crumpling its metal casing like an invisible fist. Kyler was too close to the barrel. His eardrums popped, but before deafness fell he heard screeching feedback. Dirac's mike had caught the sound and transferred it to the PA speakers throughout the track.

Moving in complete silence, hands still clamped around the screamer, Kyler recalled his unarmed combat training. He pulled on the gun and rolled backwards. Momentum carried Dirac forward; Kyler thrust his foot up against his stomach. He let go. Dirac went sailing over him, over the press box rim, out into night air. He seemed to hang suspended for a moment. Kyler leapt up in time to see him plunge into the reservoir on the statue's back.

There must've been a lot of acid in the mix. Dirac's face contorted in a silent scream. Wisps of smoke rose from his skin, already sloughing away like old paint. He tried to paddle for the side of the tank. His head dipped once, twice below the lethal brew, and disappeared completely.

So much for bringing him back alive.

Fischer leaned into his field of vision, her lips moving, but all he heard was white noise. She pointed at the ladder, made a downward motion with her hand. They descended.

Damon crouched by the stairwell. His gun bucked and casings flew as he fired at unseen targets below. Kyler rushed to join him. The crowd had battered down the door and were making a half-assed attempt at rushing the stairs, but suppression fire kept them pinned.

Kyler unslung his screamer. Two short bursts cleared the stairwell.

The ringing in his left ear gave way to a roar. He could hear words slipping in.

"—got him," Damon was saying, giving him a thumbs up. "I knew you could do it."

Fischer slapped him on the back. "I don't know if you can hear me or not, but that was one hell of a *tomoe nage*. Textbook perfect." Her eyes seemed to regard him differently. Was that respect, or just his wishful thinking?

"I can hear you. Uncle, with Dirac out of the way I don't see what's keeping us in this god-awful era."

Damon glanced over to where the dark-haired woman lay. "Me neither. We can't take the girl back with us, but I think the crowd has other things on its mind right now. Look."

The spectators had become a mob. Desert camo fought with hooded green jersey, using fists, feet, and beer bottles. Two dozen people had climbed the fence and rushed the pit where the prize truck stood on display. They overcame the monks guarding it, then turned on each other for the honor of ownership. No one seemed to be paying any attention to the battle still raging at the center of the arena, between bus and truck.

"I think these people are about to get a taste of *real* apocalypse." Kyler reached under his belt and activated the recall beacon.

BABYLON HEIST

Outside a Bronze Age sun baked the mud bricks of a thousand dwellings, beat down on the heads of slaves, soldiers, and nobles alike, dulled the bray of the onagers and parched the myriad voices of the marketplace, even hoarsened the Priest King himself, as he called out noon rites from the tallest ziggurat in the city.

But there were places the sun couldn't reach …

Beneath an abandoned temple near the hovels of Buzzard Gate, a secret chamber had been dug. Light from a clay lamp flickered in the cooling darkness. It threw shadows across the faces of three men and one woman, hunched around a table of precious cedar wood. They spoke in whispers and passed a jar brimming with black beer.

Criminals, all.

"Let me express my gratitude," said the oldest, a merchant-type with silver shekel weights woven into his white beard. "First for your being so prompt in response to my summons. Second, for having the bravery to—"

The man-mountain of a Sumerian sitting to his right let out a grunt. "Time is money. Spare us the pleasantries, Arshan, and get down to the job."

"Shumir doesn't speak for me," said the plump, painted woman seated to the old man's left. A fillet of tiny golden bells circled her brow. She wore a harness of crisscrossed threads hung with hundreds more, and there was a tinkling sound as she passed the beer. "Some of us have plenty of time."

"Ha." Shumir leveled a thick finger. "That's because your 'Temple of Holy Love' doesn't open for business until nightfall. What's a glorified whore doing here, anyway?"

Arshan cleared his throat. "I'll remind you that Iltani is a priestess. As such, she plays as vital role in our plans."

"So you keep saying." Shumir nodded at the fourth member of the group, who had yet to speak. "And what about *him*? What do we need some blonde Hellene for? 'Kyros the Eel.' I've never heard of him."

Faces swiveled to regard the foreigner.

"Well, Kyros," said Arshan, "would you like to give us an accounting of yourself?"

The slender man drew a deep breath. He'd been dreading introductions all morning. And not because he was supposedly a Macedonian Greek, who'd left his hilly homeland for the gold and intrigue of Babylon. No, Kyros the Eel, aka Kyler Knightly, field agent for

Continuity Inc., had traveled back in time more than three thousand years to get a piece of this action.

"I'd, ah, like more beer, please."

* * *

Calling the stuff "beer" was too charitable. Flat, warm, and floating with hazy chunks, you didn't drink the dark liquid so much as chew it. But alcohol was alcohol. Kyler drained the jar, stealing a glance over the rim at his companions. Like him, one of them wasn't who they appeared to be. Another time-traveler, sent back to swipe a priceless artifact for a collector in the twenty-third century. Continuity Inc. had received solid intel *what* they were after, but not *who* was involved. Finding out was Kyler's job. He'd spent several days nosing around the Babylonian underworld before he'd discovered this group. The fact they were planning something big, and soon, he took as more than a coincidence.

"The man's dry," Iltani said, noting the empty jar with a smile. She clapped her hands. "Slave! More beer."

A tall Egyptian eunuch appeared, veiled like a woman. He hustled over another jar and placed it on the table before scurrying off.

Kyler reached for the brew. Irritated with his silence, Arshan said: "Our Greek friend specializes in getting inside tight places. Hence the nickname."

"Bah." Shumir spat. "Unnecessary. With my muscles I can bore through any mud-brick wall."

"Your muscles are part of the problem," Arshan said. "Cutting a hole to fit those shoulders would take too long. And timing is crucial if we want to break into the manor of Naram Eil."

Iltani straightened. "So old Naram's our mark. What's the loot?"

Arshan and Shumir traded looks. "A tablet," the white-bearded man said at last. "A treatise on astronomy Naram keeps in his library. There's an Assyrian scholar willing to pay fifty gold minas for it—and I can probably drive him higher."

Iltani's painted face went pale. "*Fifty* gold minas …"

"I wouldn't bother putting a caper together for less," Arshan said.

The linguistic chip implanted in Kyler's mastoid process was having a hard time with Neo-Babylonian slang; words like "mark," "loot," and "caper" were criminal argot, and not in the regular lexicon. So he was several seconds behind the conversation. But he was willing to bet the "Assyrian scholar" offering the money was several thousand years in the future. And the piece of clay they were talking about was none other than the Kidinnu Tablet, a significant work of early science.

"Enough," Shumir said, looking like he wanted to spit again. He rounded on Arshan. "Whatever's going down, one thing's for certain: your fingers won't touch any of the dirty work. Not our Honest Arshan. So tell us the master plan, already."

If the old man took any offense, he didn't show it. "The plan," he said, unrolling a hide map across the table. "Now, that *is* a thing of beauty …"

* * *

After the meeting, Kyler slipped off to a shadowy bar to guzzle date wine. His nerves were still shot. Everyone he glimpsed, from the one-armed bartender to the withered old scribe sitting two stools down might be a spy for Arshan. Or Shumir. Or Iltani. They could have someone tailing him right now.

He reached down to touch the focus object he carried at his side. A bronze-headed mace, "borrowed" from the British Museum and contemporaneous with this time period. The artifact had allowed Continuity Inc.'s powerful Zygma projector to send him back circa 770 B.C. He took a measure of comfort knowing he could also use it to bash in someone's head.

"Hot day, isn't it?" the bartender said, giving him a look that could mean suspicion or nothing at all.

"It is at that."

He paid with a silver shaving and got the hell out of there. 'Hell' being an apt choice of words. The temperature in the offal-strewn streets hovered around a hundred and twenty Fahrenheit. No breeze stirred. Babylon's massive walls blocked most of the wind from the plain, and the ubiquitous mud brick trapped heat like a sponge. To make the vision complete, a huge tower straight out of Bruegel dominated the skyline, with antlike figures ascending a ramp around the exterior.

He passed a squad of soldiers in long leather capes. War season was coming up fast, and there was talk of conflict with Nineveh. He shook his head. Things never changed, did they?

A quarter-mile from Buzzard's Gate lay a smaller portal called Whore's Gate, leading to an older residential section. Kyler slunk down the adjacent alley, ready to pull his mace on any would-be muggers. He brushed aside a pile of desiccated straw to reveal a crack in the wall. A tiny roll of parchment jutted out from it.

He unrolled the message, written in Continuity Inc. cipher. Translated, it read:

NOTHING NEW ON MY END. MISS AIR CONDITIONING AND BUBBLES IN BEER. WILL RENDEVOUSZ AT THE USUAL PLACE.

Kyler's uncle Damon had been sent back under-cover as well. Communicating with him by shortwave was strictly a no-no, given that another time traveler might have a receiver. He took a stylus from his tunic and clicked out a hidden ballpoint.

IT'S GOING DOWN TONIGHT.

Message replaced, he hurried back the way he came.

* * *

"*Cops*. Into the shadows, moron."

Shumir grabbed Kyler by the arm and hauled him flat against a wall. A chariot drawn by four onagers rattled close. The soldier at the reins gripped a three-meter spear, and the scarred man crouched beside him, dressed in a corselet of bronze scales, held a compound bow. Their eyes raked the street. But the moon was a mere sliver, and the absence of lamps made Babylonian night dark as a closet. The chariot passed without slowing.

"Keep bungling," Shumir whispered, "and I'll drag your ass back to Arshan, tablet or no tablet."

"Sorry."

"Not as sorry as we'll both be if we're caught. This is the wealthy quarter, and crimes against nobility mean death."

They'd had to slink through several gates, past checkpoints and guard posts to get here. The richer portion of Babylon felt like a different city. Brick surfaces had been enameled in vibrant reds, yellows, and blues. Walls enclosed gardens of slender date palms, where unseen fountains splashed. Even the air smelled better; human waste was carted off to be dumped elsewhere. Night-blooming jasmine replaced the stink of open sewage.

They stole across a broad plaza. Shumir carried an ox-hide bag that occasionally made a clinking noise. "There's our target," he said, nodding at a walled manor nearby. "Naram Eil's place."

Kyler recalled the layout from Arshan's map. The estate boasted a tall tower, rising well above the surrounding four-meter wall. Lamplight flickered steadily at the top. Among other things, Naram Eil was an amateur astronomer.

Shumir's grin showed white against his soot-blackened face. "Stargazing as usual. Lucky for us he's got his head pointed at the sky, and not the grounds below."

They found a shadowed spot well away from any street traffic. In lieu of checking his watch, Kyler gauged the time from the moon's position. Close to midnight.

The tinkle of bells carried up the plaza. After a tense minute Kyler could make out their source; a half-dozen feminine shapes, approaching on bare feet. They'd painted their faces with talc and kohl, nude save for the jangling harnesses they wore. Iltani marched at their head. The temple prostitutes made straight for the manor's front gate. Iltani clashed a pair of cymbals together and waited, her face expectant.

"There's our distraction," Shumir said. "Move."

Kyler approached the manor wall. Gritting his teeth, he knelt on all fours and made a human table. Shumir planted a foot on his back. For a second, unbearable weight pressed against his spine. Then Shumir leapt up and caught the top of the wall. With barely a grunt, he hauled himself up one-handed. Fucking showoff. He hooked a leg over the far side and dangled his muscled arm towards Kyler. A jump, and Kyler grabbed him by the wrist. With a combination of Shumir's strength and his own scrabbling, he gained the top.

The wall was half a meter thick. Kyler pivoted on his knees to get a view of the courtyard. Young ash trees formed a walkway around a low fountain, filled with shimmering water. Just beyond he could see the inward side of the front gate and four hairy silhouettes hunkered around it. Those would be the Guti tribesmen old Naram employed as guards. They were talking in gruff voices through a small window to Iltani, on the other side. Negotiating prices.

Shumir huffed. "I guess Arshan was right about her being useful. I wouldn't care to take my chances with that lot."

Kyler nodded at the shadowed main house. "We don't have much time."

They leapt down among ferns and flowers. Shumir's bag made a muffled clank that thankfully didn't carry far. "Around back," he whispered. "Trying to force the front door puts us in view of the guards."

They circled to the rear of the house. There were no windows on the ground level, and the slits above were too narrow for even Kyler's thin frame. Ergo, they had to bore through the wall. Shumir felt along the bricks with an artist's concentration. He halted, nodding to himself, and pulled a strange tool from his bag. It had a wooden disk at one end and an auger-shaped head.

Without explanation, he thrust the bit into the wall. A turn of the disk, and the primitive drill started tearing away chunks of mud brick.

Kyler watched him work in silence, straining his ears for the sound of any approaching Guti. "This is taking too long," he whispered.

"Like hell it is. Look, I'm already through."

He pulled the drill out to reveal a small hole. From the bag he took a curved bronze rod that looked like a crowbar, and inserted it into the opening. A heave, and he levered out a brick. Someone with lesser strength would've had a harder time, but Shumir took only minutes to make a Kyler-sized opening.

"In you go," he said. "The working girls' business won't last long, so get that tablet and get out. I'll be waiting in the corner over there, behind the bush."

Leaving the hard part to me, Kyler thought. He wriggled into the jagged hole. His mace threatened to snag on a brick, but by turning his hip he managed to worm through.

Murky darkness on the other side. His palms and knees touched a floor of cool stone, smooth as marble. After a few seconds his eyes adjusted. Lamplight guttered from somewhere ahead. He crawled for it, striving to remember the layout from Arshan's map. The library was on the ground floor. A confirmed bachelor, Naram Eil kept no women. With him up in his tower and the servants asleep, the lower rooms should be vacant. That was the theory, at least.

He found a clay lamp in the foyer. Steps of polished basalt led upwards, but he skirted those, taking the lamp with him as he headed towards a hallway. The house was tomb-silent. He became too aware of his own breathing, the echo of his footfalls. If caught, he'd be punished in the most literal manner possible: his dead body would be used to shore up the hole Shumir had made. "Eye for an eye, tooth for a tooth," came directly from Hammurabi's law code, enacted in Babylon one thousand years earlier.

But there was more at stake here than his own safety. He swallowed fear and crept down the hall. At the far end, a doorway opened onto a chamber with niches carved into the walls. Clay tablets lay stacked within.

Jackpot.

Conscious of time draining away, he played lamplight over the library's shelves. There were at least a hundred tablets, all crowded with wedge-shaped cuneiform. Not a large selection by modern standards, but enough to take too long if he wasn't careful. Luckily, he had an excellent reference hidden in his homespun tunic. A copy of the Kidinnu Tablet, exact as they could make it in the twenty-third century, after sections had crumbled away. Using the copy as a guide, he shuffled through tablets until he found a match. The real one went into his tunic along with the fake. Ironic, but the best way to protect it for now was to keep it close. Arshan and crew would receive the copy. Kyler would then return the tablet to Naram Eil, after he'd nabbed his time-traveling thief.

Satisfied, he turned to the doorway. And froze.

A sleek black leopard had come padding into the room. The beast sat on its haunches, observing him with lambent yellow eyes. A silver collar encircled its thick neck.

Kyler silently cursed. Arshan's plans hadn't allowed for pets.

The leopard let out a growl. It might be playful, or it might be a prelude to ripping his guts open. He considered the mace at his side, but he didn't really want to brain the beautiful animal. Also, killing this far back in time was frowned on; even the loss of a big cat could snowball into unforeseen consequences.

The leopard got up and slunk over. It nuzzled his hand before growling again, louder this time. Slow as he could, Kyler withdrew the stylus he'd used in the alley. Two strong clicks. Instead of a ballpoint, an eight gauge hypodermic slid from the tip.

The cat's growl edged into a roar. Black lips pulled back over bared incisors. He plunged the needle into its neck. The stylus hissed, injecting a full reservoir of toxin. Paralytics designed for a ninety-kilogram man made the leopard's muscles spasm. It went rigid before keeling over.

Kyler's heart started to pound. Could someone have heard all that growling? He left the lamp where he'd set it down and hurried from the library. Passing the foyer, he glimpsed a stooped figure coming around a corner at the top of the stairs. He dove for the smooth-floored chamber. A short distance away gaped the hole Shumir had made. He ploughed through without getting stuck.

Out into the gardens. Compared to the house's dark interior, it seemed almost bright. But where was Shumir? He searched the shadowed corner where he'd said he'd be waiting. No trace.

Rustling noises. A pair of broad-shouldered shapes came loping down the side of the house. Their interlude with Iltani's 'maidens' must be over. Kyler pressed himself against the ground.

An old man's voice cried out from the front of the house. The guards wheeled and started running in that direction. Naram must've already found the leopard. They'd search the house, find the hole, and find *him*, a short distance away.

He leapt for the wall's rim, but couldn't reach it. Goddamn Shumir. He must've known he would've left him trapped here—

Wait a second. How would Shumir have gotten out? He wasn't any taller.

Kyler felt along the wall. His fingers brushed a deep gouge in the brick, at the perfect height for a foothold. Shumir could've made it with one of his tools. He thrust his toes inside, pushed, and scrambled over the top of the wall. Hang-dropped to the other side.

The open plaza stretched around him. Instead of feeling relief, the back of his neck prickled. He sensed eyes watching from the darkness.

Kyler had been a Level Two Precognitive before becoming a field agent. His intuitions had a habit of turning into solid facts. And right now, his intuition screamed to leap for cover.

He did so. Two meters to his left a public fountain bubbled, and he hurled himself behind it.

His retinas flashed. A finger of ruby-red sparks angled down to touch the space he'd just vacated. It scorched a pattern on the paving stones and followed to where he crouched. There was a *whoosh* as the fountain's water converted to steam.

Someone had brought a laser to ancient Babylon. He rolled and popped his head up. Again, the ruby light flashed, and he ducked. This time the whooshing went on for a long moment, as the gunner raked the fountain. Either excited or frustrated. Steam rose in a large, roiling cloud.

Kyler stood up. When the beam flashed again it struck the cloud and diffracted into a harmless spray of color. Smoke would've been more effective, but what the hell. He traced the laser's path to a wall top some thirty meters away.

The beam winked out. Likely, the capacitor needed several seconds to charge again.

Likely.

But if he stayed here, pinned, his sniper would find another angle.

Expecting to be fried at any moment, he broke from the fountain and ran.

* * *

Twice Kyler got lost bolting down darkened side-streets and alleys. Twice he had to retrace his steps. Soldiers, cesspools, and staggering drunks seemed to materialize out of the warm night air. He eluded them all.

The twisting streets began to look familiar. Another few blocks and he found his safe house; a bottom floor room in a four-story tenement. He had to wake the landlord by pounding on the door, which got him a sharp look, but thankfully, no questions. His room was a tiny cubicle with a straw tick and the Babylonian equivalent of a chamber pot. A slit-window let in air. During the day, the place was an oven.

He rolled up the tick and placed the tablet—the real one—in a niche he'd dug the day before. Hopefully, Damon would have access to a better hiding place. Loot secured, he collapsed into a corner and allowed himself the luxury of several deep breaths.

Safe. For now, anyways. Nothing like a leopard or a laser-potting sniper to remind of one's mortality. He fought the urge to reach under his tunic and activate the recall beacon clipped there. A quantum-entangled signal could haul him back to the present in minutes.

But that would mean leaving Uncle Damon high and dry. And there was still the matter of the mystery-thief.

Though he had a damn good idea who it was.

* * *

Babylon came to life in the ash-colored dawn. The sun had risen early for another day of merciless scorching, throwing shadows across the abandoned temple. As Kyler approached, he could hear the echoes of stalls being erected in the market near Buzzard Gate. Commerce never waited long.

He crept into the temple courtyard, eyes wary. Arshan's plan called for a regroup the morning after the heist, to exchange the tablet. It had struck Kyler as the perfect opportunity for a double-cross.

But some of his tension eased when he spied Shumir waiting in plain sight. The big man leaned against a cracked stone altar, his arms folded. He grinned at Kyler. "Glad to see you made it."

"No thanks to you."

"Hey now, don't get hostile." Shumir was keeping his right hand tucked behind his back. "Sorry I had to ditch you in the garden, but those tribesmen were loose."

"Where's Arshan?"

"Not here yet. You got the tablet, right?"

"You going to try and laser me for it again?"

To his credit, Shumir's face remained calm. "I don't know what you're talking about."

"Sure you don't. Two things you need to know, pal. One, I've hidden the tablet in a secure place. Two, I didn't come back in time alone. My uncle Damon's armed and watching us right now."

That last part was a bluff, but it sounded good.

"Alright," Shumir said in Anglic, stretching to show the auto-pistol in his right hand. "How'd you figure it?"

"Your muscles. They don't have deltoid grafting in the ancient Middle East. Another thing; minus the extra pigment and the hook someone added to your nose, you look just like a professional wrestler from a couple years back. Big Hoss McAdams, I think his name was."

"Big *Boss* McAdams. But close enough."

"One thing I don't get. If you brought a laser back, why bother with all the subtleties? You could've roasted Naram's guards from the wall, and burned through his front door."

McAdams shook his head. "That would blow my cover to any other time travelers. No, I had to take a low-tech approach."

"Until you tried to shoot me, anyway."

"Nothing personal."

Kyler felt his hands clench. "You've got no idea what you're doing. The Kidinnu Tablet's a big chunk of early science. Steal it, and we could be travelling back to a radically different future."

"Bullshit. I don't buy any of that 'paradox' theory. You're just another government agent trying to suppress the free market."

"More bullshit."

McAdams's voice grew reasonable. "Look, I bet you're getting paid dick for this mission. Some bureaucrat's salary. My employer can triple it. Quadruple it, even. Just tell me where—"

A bearded figure appeared at the edge of the courtyard, silhouetted in the morning sun. "By the breath of Utuk," Arshan said, "what language are you two speaking? It sounds like goats farting."

McAdams's gun slithered out of sight. "Just an old Greek dialect I picked up. Kyros here found the tablet."

"Of course he did."

"I guess it's time to divvy, then," McAdams said, winking at Kyler.

"Not quite. Iltani isn't here, yet. And I'll need the tablet first, to obtain the full sum ..."

As he spoke, a dozen men converged on the courtyard from different directions. Ragged men, lean as hyenas, gripping sickle-bladed swords and knives. Babylonian gutter-trash. They shuffled past Arshan to form a ring around Kyler and McAdams.

"What gives?" the big man said. "I was the one who told you about the buyer. I approached you to set this whole thing up."

51

"I found a new buyer," Arshan said.

Kyler pulled the copy from his tunic. "What if I just gave you the tablet right now? Would you let us go?"

Arshan shook his head. "Sadly, my new buyer wants no traces on his end. So you'll both have to disappear." He nodded to his cutthroats.

Kyler held the fake high, threatening to break it. But McAdams had already leveled his gun. The automatic barked. Two thugs dropped as explosive bullets tore holes in their chests. The others hesitated, unfamiliar with the strange weapon. McAdams cut down two more while they gawked.

"Clip's dry," he said, in Anglic.

"The secret room." Kyler reached behind the altar and yanked up the concealed trapdoor. Below lay semi-darkness. He leapt down without bothering to use the ladder. McAdams joined him seconds later.

The cedar wood table was still there, and someone had re-lit the lamp. Breathing hard, McAdams glanced at the bright square in the ceiling. "We're trapped in here, you know."

"They can only come at us from one direction."

Above, Arshan's voice exhorted his men to finish the job. Shadows hunched over the trapdoor. McAdams grabbed up the table. He tilted it forward and charged as a trio of men dropped down. Wood slammed them against the wall with bone-jarring force.

"Just like in the ring!" McAdams's shouted. "I'll break your primitive little—"

A thug landed on top of him, knife slashing. McAdams hurled the man to the floor. Blood dripped from a deep cut across his pectorals.

Another thug leapt down.

Frowned on or not, Kyler would have to fight, and probably kill, to get out of this alive. He hefted the mace—and caught a faint jingling, behind him. Sharp bronze pressed against his throat.

"Not so fast, handsome," Iltani's voice husked. "Tell me you've got the tablet."

He had to speak carefully, to keep the blade from cutting his Adam's apple. "I've got it. But Arshan will kill you, too."

"Maybe. Maybe not. I'm very persuasive." She took her lips away from his ear. "Ahmose, search him."

A pair of hands felt through his tunic. Kyler could only watch as McAdams fought off three armed men at once. He dislocated a jaw with a single punch, but got a knife in the thigh for his trouble.

The Egyptian eunuch's hands found the tablet and tore it free.

"Alright then," said Iltani. "I've got my bargaining chip. Tell me one good reason why I shouldn't slit your throat right now."

"You have a deep-felt love for humanity?"

The knife bit tighter. "Try again."

"How about this: your eunuch is actually my uncle Damon Cole in disguise, sent back in time from the twenty-third century."

"*What*?"

There was the familiar hiss of a narcoject, and the pressure against Kyler's throat slackened. He turned to see Ahmose/Damon pull a stylus from Iltani's neck. Her rigid body crashed to the floor.

"Your timing, as ever, is impeccable."

Damon tore the veil off his face. Like McAdams, he'd had extra pigmentation implanted. "For your sake, maybe. Not your friend's."

Behind them, McAdams had just finished throttling the last of his attackers. Both men went down in each other's arms. A knife hilt protruded from McAdams's muscled back, near the base of his spine. He convulsed, and a throaty death-rattle filled the chamber.

"*Requiescat in pace*, Big Boss," Kyler said.

"Did you find out who he was working for?"

Kyler shook his head. "The least of our troubles. Arshan's waiting up there and I figure he's still got a couple swordsmen left. We can't activate the recall signal until we've returned the real tablet to Naram Eil."

"Gloom and doom, nephew." Damon fished an egg-shaped object out of his robes. "You really need to put more faith in technology."

"What's that?"

"Gas grenade." A grin split his darkened face. "Non-lethal, but when Arshan and his men wake up they'll have splitting headaches. Too bad aspirin won't be invented for a couple millennia."

†

STRONTIUM DREAMS

Mac met up with Lev in the quays of Jetsam Flats, just as the soot-streaked sky was lightening from purple. He'd been living outside for two weeks, still learning how to sleep with a respirator on.

Which was why he felt dead-tired and never saw the Collection team until they pounced.

He'd come strolling up, Lev beside him. Their confederate, Cal, was waiting as agreed, leaning against a plastic-covered mound only inches from the water. Cal with his arms folded, his hood pulled forward and trying to look nonchalant. Like the three of them didn't have Big Plans for the morning.

Then he felt it. Instant roiling in his guts. And just as his knees folded and dropped him to the filth, he thought, Oh shit, because he'd had the sensation before, and knew what a non-lethal ambush meant. Cal and Lev were writhing, too.

Half a dozen men came boiling out from behind a midden heap, each one encased in armor. Mac scoped them as Independents by the artwork stenciled on the ceramic plating; ochre vulture skulls and crossbones, against gold-flecked black. One of them clutched a wide beam maser with a square barrel. Mac figured that was the weapon that had laid him out.

They came to him first, kicked his hood away, and took one look at the ideogram stamped on his forehead. Moved on, muttering curses beneath their faceplates. Mac's breathing calmed a little. Next came Lev, but they could see his indigo-mottled skin without much prodding and gave him a pass, too.

Cal, poor bastard—not his lucky day. One Collector pinioned his arms and the other tore his respirator off. Cal's goiter glowed cherry red under his swollen neck, a sure tag of thyroid cancer, but it must've been lean times in the collection business, because they popped him with a hypo anyway, started laying his slack body out on a folding gurney. The guy with the hypo complained their haul wasn't worth the joules it took for a maser shot.

Mac had recovered a little in the meanwhile. Enough, if he wanted, to fling himself up and try something stupid. Like bouncing a shiv off all that hard armor. Or trying to wrestle well-fed, gene-modified goons who outnumbered him six to one. So he stayed right where he was.

A glance at Lev's flat eyes told him his friend was thinking the same thing.

And for maybe the thousandth time in his young life, he thanked his father for blowing the last of the family money on the Genetic Undesirables stamp gracing his forehead, a five-armed logo warning of tainted nucleotides and dangerous recessives. The GU rating made his organs worthless and kept his flesh out of the Long Pork tacos hawked on every corner of Jetsam Flats.

He lay sprawled there, waiting, until the team hauled Cal away.

Lev helped him to his feet. "Well, more for us, I guess."

* * *

They tore the plastic off the mound. Underneath sat a five-foot thick slab of styrocore, lashed with tubing to protect the edges. Mac looked the thing over and frowned. "Not much of a raft."

"Cal talked it up, alright," Lev said. "Where's the fucking pole?"

Finding it took half an hour. Mac saw the end of a pipe sticking out of the same heap the Collectors had been hiding behind and drew it out. The pipe kept coming, and didn't stop until he had about fifteen feet in his hands.

"Long enough, at least," Lev said.

The raft was Cal's contribution to their venture. Lev knew the location. And Mac had been invited along, his friendship with Lev notwithstanding, this was business, because he could hit a pigeon on the wing with nothing more than a strip of cloth and a rock. He'd been bagging meat this way for the Sal Goynes Co-Opt since the age of ten, and would've continued doing so but for the dissolution of said Co-Opt about a month ago, dumping him on the street.

They'd been running low on pigeons, anyways.

Mac and Lev shouldered the raft into the Soup. It bobbed there for a moment, looking none too seawor- thy, and it took some coaxing from Lev for Mac to crawl aboard. The Styrocore dipped immediately under their weight, stopping about a hands-breadth from the glossy water. Lev rose to his feet, cautious, and used the pole to push them from the quay.

* * *

Lev poled. Mac uncoiled his sling, a ghetto weapon made from two braided cords and a pouch in the center. He laid out six bullets of scavenged lead for quick use.

The sky turned lavender and dumped benzene- mingled rain on their heads.

When the clouds cleared up, so did the Soup. Mac could look over the side and see the pole refracting down, pushing against the detritus of a hundred genera- tions. God knew what was all heaped down there. A couple years ago there'd been rumors of cannibal fish that could force themselves up from the water, flop around long enough to snare children, but Mac knew that was bullshit. Nothing organic could survive in the Soup. And if mutant life was to somehow flourish, everybody and their dog would be out on the water with nets, fishing it back to extinction.

Which reminded him how hungry he was.

"Heads up," Lev said.

They'd poled far enough out that Jetsam Flats was just a jagged silhouette promising wickedness. The floating trash piles were giving way to a forest of girders and crossbeams jutting from the rainbow-slicked Soup. About fifty feet ahead a beam slanted low over the water, thick enough for several people to stand on or take cover by lying prone. And yup, as he watched, a thin shape popped up as if to get a better view of the raft and ducked back down. The shape had been holding a short spear looped to its' wrist.

"Children of Entropy, what do you bet?" Lev said.

"They got atl-atl's."

Mac fitted a thumb-sized bullet to the sling's pouch. He stood up, legs spread akimbo on the shifting surface. At forty feet he whipped the sling in an overhand arc and loosed at the precise moment. The bullet spanged against a crossbeam, the metal striking so hard it flattened and stuck there.

Lev pulled his respirator off. "More where that came from, motherfuckers," he shouted, cupping a hand around his mouth. "Just show your heads again, give my friend something to hit."

Nobody did.

* * *

"We lost Cal, risked that shit back there, for this?"

"Just watch."

Lev had guided them to the gutted core of a sky-scraper, clogged with trash. Polycrete chunks, cracked open and barring fang-like ribs of rusted metal, surrounded the ruin, threatening to impale the raft if they tried to moor it.

"What am I supposed to be watching?"

"That part. There." Lev pointed.

Mac followed his gesture to a wicked cluster of spikes, spitting distance from the raft. Watched. For a minute, nothing. Then the spikes warped. They seemed to melt, droop away at impossible angles, flickered. Then they were spikes again.

Lev thrust the pole at the cluster. It passed through with no resistance.

"Hologram," he said. "I spotted it two months back, working another job for Slim Jim Beck. We were out here on a proper skiff, not like this piece of shit. I saw the flicker and thought my eyes were playing tricks, but it happened again. I didn't tell anyone else on the crew, just figured I'd come back later and see what that thing was hiding."

"Good call."

"What do you think?"

"Got to be something," Mac said, looking at the phantom spikes. "They can't make holograms anymore."

Lev pushed the raft towards the cluster. A three-foot claw of corroded steel reached for Mac's face, and illusion or not, he had to fight to keep from ducking. He shut his eyes. When he opened them again he saw a crazy matrix of criss-crossed golden threads, then darkness, then sudden light as the raft passed into an open space.

The hologram, and the ruined walls of the skyscraper, concealed a vast interior bowl of poured polycrete. Not new, but not dilapidated like the outside. In the bowl's center, a tower rose from the lapping Soup, covered with massive intake vents.

"Industrial, I think," Lev said.

Not what Mac had expected. But the structure looked intact, the intake vents were humming, sucking in poison air, and something had to be powering them. Ergo, the tower must have shit worth stealing.

Lev poled them closer, and they made a circuit of the tower's base. There was no obvious way in. However, one of the lower vents stayed quiet while the others around it whooshed, and Mac, after standing on Lev's back and hauling himself up by the vent's rusted lip, saw why. The fan blades inside weren't moving. Behind them, angling down into the darkness, gaped an air shaft wide enough to accommodate a man.

Lev cut tubing from the side of the raft using a ceramic knife, and tossed one end up to Mac, who tied it around a frozen fan blade. The raft moored, Lev bent and leapt for the vent's lip. He caught it with one hand and Mac pulled him up by seizing the other. They crouched in the circular space, listening. More humming drifted up from the shaft. Lev gave Mac a hard look and drew his knife from beneath his parka. He started to crawl down the shaft, keeping the blade clutched in his hand. Mac tied the sling's cords around his arm, drew his own shiv, and followed.

* * *

They got maybe twelve feet. The shaft turned into flexible tubing, and the plastic, fragile with dry-rot, ripped beneath them. Mac tumbled for the space of a second before hard metal reached up and slammed his tailbone. The shiv went flying. He heard Lev cuss nearby and groped for him, because they'd been plunged into semi-darkness.

First thing he noticed, after touching the reassurance of Lev's parka, was the air quality. When you went inside a structure with intact pumps and filters the taint level was supposed to drop. But the HUD in Mac's respirator still read amber, the same as outside conditions on a typical day.

Second thing he noticed, as his eyes adjusted, were the rows of human-sized silhouettes surrounding them.

Lev rolled to his feet, knife ready. Mac looked around in the dimness for his weapon and couldn't find it. But the human shapes didn't converge. In fact, they remained stock-still.

"Listen," Lev said.

Gasping sounds. The whirr and click of complicated machines.

Mac got up and inspected the closest figure. It was human, all right. Gender hard to tell because of the shaved head, emaciated chest, and series of tubes and hoses gobbling the body below the waist. He figured it was a guy. A vertical framework kept him standing and bound his limbs. His head drooped, but Mac heard him sucking breath through his mouth—and here was a special horror—he was breathing without any filter or mask, just taking in that raw sewage, straight. Oddly, there was some kind of apparatus covering his nose, connected by two snake-like tubes running into the floor. But since the guy seemed to be exhaling into that, Mac didn't see what good it would do.

Lev joined him. He looked at the living corpse slumped there, then at the rows of similarly bound-and-tubed figures, receding into the darkness. "How many …?"

At his voice, the figure stirred. He raised his head and his eyes were hallways with no doors and no lights at the end.

"Jesus, Lev. Cut his throat and do him a favor."

"You gentlemen touch my property," a voice behind them said, "and I'll burn you where you stand."

* * *

There were two of them.

Man-Plus types, a modified offshoot Mac had thought extinct, but here they were, all seven feet of them. Lean, even by ghetto standards, with rope-like muscles and grotesque endowments. The latter obvious because besides respirators, they wore only harness. Glittering tools and bone-fetishes hung from the black plastic straps. The slightly taller of the two pointed a maser at them.

The narrow-barreled kind. The kind that seared neat holes in people instead of making them nauseous.

"Step closer, please," he said.

Mac and Lev did so.

Two pairs of spider-hands seized them, snatched Lev's knife, frisked their parkas for further weapons and found none. The shorter freak laughed the whole time. There was an involuntary quality about it. His long limbs shook and his face twitched, and Mac remembered an outbreak of Kuru that had raged through Jetsam Flats one year, when the vendors had been mixing too much nervous tissue with the long pork. Something like that must have happened to this guy.

Not that he felt sorry for him.

"You two broke into the wrong establishment," Taller Freak said.

The shorter one stopped giggling long enough to say: "I told you the hologram's gone wonky."

"I'll fix it when I fix it."

More laughter. Taller cocked his head to one side like he was thinking. "Alright, you're coming down with us. We can figure out your punishment later, after—"

Mac saw Lev tense at 'punishment.' He started to bolt. Where the hell he could bolt to was a good question, but it didn't stop him. Tall Freak's bare foot lashed out. It connected with the back of Lev's knee and down he went.

The maser, Mac noticed, stayed level the whole time.

* * *

Down with us meant being prodded, shoved, and finally dragged into a cage-lift that made ominous creaking noises as it dropped. At some point in their descent the cage passed through a violent cross-current of air and the HUD in Mac's respirator blinked from amber to green. The lift shuddered to a stop. They filed out into a circular chamber crammed with electronics, furniture, tools, food, banks of monitor screens, and hospital beds with red-rusted sheets and worn straps.

Mac couldn't help staring at those.

The Freak Brothers removed their masks and hung them on a peg, then gestured for Mac and Lev to do the same. Mac took his off slow, bracing for the smell he'd learned to expect from sealed environments.

Surprise. The air smelled clean.

"Don't get much of that on the outs, do you?" Taller Freak said. He snuffed in a lungful. "Fresh. That's what we make here. Fresh air. Those zombies up top, they take it in, scrub the crap out with their own lungs. We route the CO_2 down into a tank of pre-Soup algae, and the result, well, you're breathing it."

"Lot of demand for good air," Shorter Freak added.

Which made Mac's stomach hitch a little, thinking where the oxygen was coming from. But Jesus, it was fresh.

"Anyone with a filter can scrub air," Lev said. He'd taken off his respirator and was rubbing his knee.

"Yeah, but that shit's flat," Taller Freak said. "Tasteless. You ever have spring water? It's got minerals and other organic compounds that give it flavor. Re-processed water, that's all been leeched out. Air's the same way."

"What the fuck's spring water?" Lev said.

"Never mind. You Soup Rats get your clothes off, and onto those beds. It's exam time."

"I thought we were going to be punished," Mac said.

"Exactly."

* * *

They stripped them, bound them to the gore-crusted beds, and probed.

Mac shut his eyes and thought about pigeons.

"Why's that one got purple skin?"

"It's not a mutation. Fungal symbiot, injected directly beneath the stratum corneum. Life cycle of the fungus provides extra adenosine, decreasing the need for food intake. The practice's unpopular for cosmetic reasons."

"Ah. What about the GU marker on this guy?"

Something cold and sharp dug into Mac's forehead. "Fake."

He cracked an eyelid. Taller Freak crouched over him, so close he could smell his slaughterhouse breath. The shorter one hung back, holding the maser. He had, Mac noticed, an enormous erection.

God, he wished he hadn't noticed that.

"What're you going to do with us?" he said.

Taller Freak showed him a mouth of spade-like teeth. "We're trying to determine if you'd make good filters. That's one option. The other option is we eat you. Assuming it's safe, of course."

"Safety first," Shorter Freak said.

No.

Mac hurled what strength he had left against the straps. They didn't budge. He tensed for a second attempt, but a giant fist slammed down without warning, the knuckles grazing his temple. He saw gray with flashes of white and the bed spun. Third try. He thrashed again. The straps came loose like magic, and he fell. Laughter.

"Okay," Taller said, "that's not the first thing we're going to do."

"No, not the first."

"You cover him. I'll get protection. No telling where that's been."

Mac pushed himself up. Shorter Freak hovered within kicking range, almost straddling him. He had the maser trained on his forehead. Out the corner of his eye, Mac could see Lev wriggling on the bed, still bound. Mac's clothes lay heaped a couple feet from his right hand, including the sling and bullets. The Freak Brothers hadn't recognized it as a weapon.

If he could reach—

Shorter Freak started laughing.

His whole body shook; his lungs filled and spasmed again. Shorter seemed to fight it, gritting his teeth, trying to keep the maser steady. But the Kuru played fuck with his nerves. He guffawed and his eyes rolled up in his head. The gun drifted wide.

Mac grabbed the sling, shoved a bullet in the pouch, and whirled it without releasing. The lead smacked into Shorter's eyesocket. Pulped it. Still laughing, Shorter clawed at the wound with his free hand. Mac seized the maser and tore it free. He jabbed the gun in Shorter's general direction, squeezing the firing stud three times.

Shorter stopped laughing.

"What, are you at him already?" came Taller's voice. "I thought I said—"

He appeared from behind a stack of boxes, holding a canister of spray-on prophylactic. Mac shot him.

His hand convulsed against the trigger and the barrel jerked from left to right. The beam's swath burned the top off Taller's head.

* * *

They threw sheets over the bodies.

A glance at the monitors showed what Mac had already suspected: the Freak Brothers, aside from their prisoners, were the only inhabitants. Mac and Lev had the complex to themselves.

"Makes you kind of wonder, doesn't it?" Lev said.

"Wonder what?"

"These two." He pointed at the corpses under the sheets, still smoking and fouling the air with the familiar sweetness of cooked flesh. "Did they build this tower? Or did they just sneak in like we did, kill the owners, and take over. "

"Who cares?"

"I do. Maybe new people keep cycling through here, in a loop. Like the air."

"You're getting way too fucking metaphysical. Let's toss the place."

First thing they scavenged was food. Mac skipped the cartons of fibrous gray meat, tagging them as questionable, and crunched his way through six cans of bamboo shoots in soy protein broth. He found a container marked 'solvent' full of clear, alcohol-smelling liquid and had at that. Lev joined him. Stomachs full, heads lolling in glorious intoxication, they settled onto reclining chairs scaled for giants.

"Okay, good score," Lev said, his voice slurred. "But what about those people up there? We can't just … leave them plugged in, like that."

"No." Maybe it was his sudden change in fortune, but Mac felt a throb of humanity. Or maybe it was just the solvent. "I say mercy kill. We figure out how the life support works, then shut the whole grid off."

"Agreed."

"But later, alright? I want to enjoy this."

"You keeping the gun?"

Mac patted the hard lump stashed in his pocket. "Mine by right of combat."

"Ah, crap," Lev said, and his eyelids fluttered. Less than a minute later the bootleg alcohol had rocked him to sleep.

About the Author

 Garnett Elliott lives and works in Tucson, Arizona. He's had stories appear in *Alfred Hitchcock's Mystery Magazine*, *Needle: A Magazine of Noir*, *Reloaded (Both Barrels 2)*, *Uncle B's Drive-In Fiction*, *Blood and Tacos*, *Battling Boxing Stories*, and numerous online magazines and print anthologies.

ALSO BY GARNETT ELLIOTT
FROM BEAT TO A PULP BOOKS
www.beattoapulp.com

Superpowers clash on the deadliest planet in the solar system ...

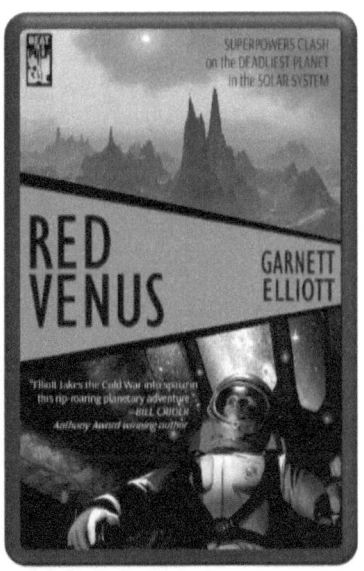

Fog-shrouded Venus had refused to give up her mysteries, until the USSR sent their best and brightest on a top-secret scientific mission. Now the crew of the Krasnyy Sokol, led by gorgeous Cosmonaut Nadezhda Gura, must brave a hellish hothouse of jungle swampland crawling with monstrous life. It's Russians and rayguns against a death planet-and that's before the Americans show up.

At 17K words, RED VENUS is a slam-bang trip on atomic-powered rockets, seen through the eyes of the East. Read it, tovarisch, and experience a part of the solar system that never was.

A fistful of East on West Mayhem ...

It's 1866. The Civil War is over and no-account grifter Carson Lowe pays a visit to the bustling Gold Rush city of San Francisco. But instead of quick riches he finds big trouble in and under a fledgling Chinatown, when a Taoist immortal threatens to wake the ... Dragon by the Bay!

Is it a western? Or a kung fu story with all the earth-shaking action of a Shaw Brothers' flick? It's both, as well as a homage to John Carpenter's Big Trouble in Little China. Weighing in at 22K words, this lean novelette delivers a fistful of East on West mayhem sure to crack a few smiles-- and ribs--before it's over.

A collection of Southwestern crime tales ...

The Border ... an alkaline limbo between two worlds, where desperation and violence loom like the ever-present sun. Scorched Noir takes a blistering look at crime along the desert *corridos*, the creosote bushes and dead *arroyos* where only scorpions thrive. Eight tales in the triple-digits by hardboiled author Garnett Elliott. From organ smugglers to drug-crazed *brujas*, this is one collection of Southwestern noir you don't want to miss. *Caliente!*

The Lizard's Ardent Uniform
WHERE KYLER KNIGHTLY AND DAMON COLE BEGAN

"All that we see or seem, is but a dream within a dream."
—*Edgar Allan Poe*

The Lizard's Ardent Uniform and Other Stories, from Veridical Dreams Vol. I, takes you on several voyages into every day nightmares, bizarre detours, and hellish worlds. Enlisting the talents of authors Chris F. Holm (*Ellery Queen Mystery Magazine*), Terrie Farley Moran (*Well Read, Then Dead*), Patti Abbott (*Home Invasion*), Evan V. Corder, Steve Weddle (*Needle: A Magazine of Noir*), Hilary Davidson (*The Damage Done*), and Garnett Elliott (*Alfred Hitchcock Mystery Magazine*), thought-provoking fragments from the dream journals of Kyle J. Knapp (writer and poet of *Pluvial Gardens* and *Celebrations in the Ossuary*, who passed away in 2013 at the age of twenty-three) are fleshed out into seven stirring tales of crime, science fiction, literary, and fantasy. Edited and with an introduction by BEAT to a PULP's David Cranmer.

Stories include:

The Lizard's Ardent Uniform — Chris F. Holm
Dust to Dust — Terrie Farley Moran
Twin Talk — Patti Abbott
The Malignant Reality — Evan V. Corder (including "The Needles" poem by Kyle J. Knapp)
Ghosts in the Fog — Steve Weddle
The Debt — Hilary Davidson
The Zygma Gambit — Garnett Elliott

A portion of the proceeds from this collection will go to higher education.

GARNETT ELLIOTT stories
from the Drifter Detective series:

THE DRIFTER DETECTIVE

Jack Laramie, grandson of the legendary US Marshal Cash Laramie, is a tough-as-nails WWII vet roaming the modern West. He lives out of a horse trailer hitched to the back of a DeSoto, searching out PI gigs to keep him afloat. With his car limping along, Jack barely makes it to the sleepy town of Clyde, Texas, where he stops at a garage. While waiting for repairs, he accepts a job from the sheriff, pulling surveillance on a local oilman allegedly running liquor to Indian reservations in Oklahoma. When Jack runs afoul of several locals and becomes dangerously close to the oilman's hot-to-trot wife, he wonders if the money is worth his life. Garnett Elliott writes in the best hardboiled tradition of the masters and turns out a tour-de-force novelette.

HELL UP IN HOUSTON

Houston has been called "a sprawling city of astronauts and cowboys, in the middle of a swamp." And now Jack Laramie, rural-wandering PI, is headed up that way after his faithless Desoto blows its radiator. Jack's got a bit of a past with the city, in the form of a Cajun PI named Lameaux—a guy who mixes his "investigations" with organized vice. So Jack decides to lay low, holing up in a swanky downtown hotel called the Fulton. It's a splurge after sleeping in an old horse trailer night after night, but Jack figures he deserves a break. Until the Fulton's grizzled house detective shows up with a proposition … Jack's way out of his league this time around, and when he discovers a blackmailing scheme involving a famous industrialist, he finds himself bumping gun-barrels with the Federal Government. Survival's going to require throwing the PI code out the window. And some quick thinking. Join Cash Laramie's hardluck grandson in this second installment of The Drifter Detective series.

GIRLS OF BUNKER PINES

Jack Laramie's back in the third installment of the "Drifter Detective" series. This time he's parked his horse trailer "beyond the pine curtain" in East Texas, where he makes the acquaintance of a troubled Korean War veteran—and a pair of vivacious burlesque dancers, with their hands in a long con game gone wrong. Atom Age paranoia meets booze, buckshot, and buxom babes, as Jack struggles to save a wayward soul who doesn't want saving, and scraps with an unlikely enforcer from the Dallas Mob. This Drifter offers riveting glimpses of Jack's past, including the last moments of the B-17 Black Betty, and the depredations of Stalag Luft Three. One warning: this is also the hardest-boiled, and features an ending not for the faint of heart.

DINERO DEL MAR

Jack Laramie finds himself in the middle of a rural beauty contest that's as crooked as a busted fiddle. Things get worse from there, and a chance encounter in the Corpus Christi drunk-tank leads to a new case-on Texas's dazzling Padre Island. A big, old mansion full of scheming rich folks, lawyers, and psychics is just the beginning. Jack survives the 'trip' of his life, but is his craftiness a match for the privileged upper crust? Dinero Del Mar is the longest Drifter to date, and features an ending that will forever change the series. Don't miss it!

Look for more short stories by Garnett Elliott in these collections from BEAT to a PULP:

"Ransom and Red Fingers"

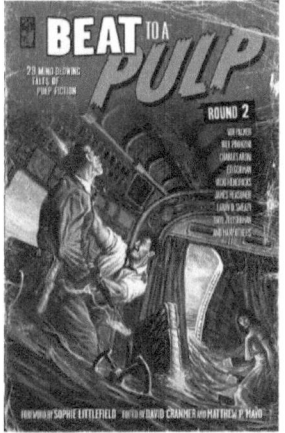

in *BEAT to a PULP: Round Two* Smoke 'em if you got 'em, then set your jaw and steel your stance, 'cause BEAT to a PULP: Round Two is here! It's all meat, no filler in this red-raw-and-oozing collection of twenty-nine tales of pure pulp action. You'll find aliens, gangsters, drifters, mountain men, private dicks, gun molls, loners, misfits, drunks, thugs, booze-hounds, and more, all brawling in the pages of Round Two. This powerhouse compilation doles out the genres, from hardboiled crime, western, and noir to sci-fi, fantasy, literary, horror, and more.

"Phantom Black and the Big Wide Open"

in *BEAT to a PULP: Superhero* What makes a superhero? Someone with special powers … Ordinary people doing good deeds … Anyone with sophisticated technological gadgets and incredible agility? Superheroes can spring up from the most unexpected people in the most unusual places, and BEAT to a PULP: Superhero has gathered some of the best hardboiled and noir crime stories with a superhero bend.

Offering short story collections and novellas in a variety of genres (from noir and hardboiled crime to Westerns, from science fiction to the undefinable), BEAT to a PULP is sure to have something for every pulp enthusiast. See what's new in our catalog from some of the finest pulp writers of today.

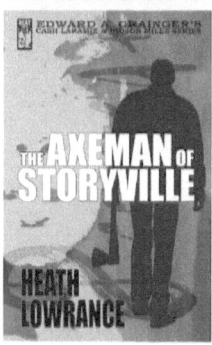  

www.beattoapulp.com